Charles Townsend

Rio Grande

An Original Drama in Three Acts

Charles Townsend

Rio Grande
An Original Drama in Three Acts

ISBN/EAN: 9783743389007

Manufactured in Europe, USA, Canada, Australia, Japa

Cover: Foto ©Andreas Hilbeck / pixelio.de

Manufactured and distributed by brebook publishing software
(www.brebook.com)

Charles Townsend

Rio Grande

An Original Drama in Three Acts

BY

CHARLES TOWNSEND

AUTHOR OF "SPY OF GETTYSBURG" "UNCLE JOSH" "THE WOVEN WEB" "BOR
DER LAND" "EARLY VOWS" "DECEPTION" "ON GUARD" "MISS
MADCAP" "BROKEN FETTERS" "SHAUN AROON" "THE
FAMILY DOCTOR" "A BREEZY CALL" ETC.

AUTHOR'S EDITION

BOSTON

CHARACTERS.

JOSE SEGURA, *a wealthy Spanish-American.*
COL. LAWTON, *commanding the garrison.*
CAPT. PAUL WYBERT, *a junior officer.*
JUDGE BIGGS, *an enthusiastic citizen.*
LIEUT. CADWALLADER, *an " American aristocrat," and a holiday soldier.*
JOHNNIE BANGS, *a dime-novel desperado.*
CORPORAL CASEY, *an old " vet."*
RETTA, *Segura's niece, in love with Paul.*
SOPHIA, *Lawton's daughter, betrothed to Paul.*
MAMIE, *Johnnie's sister, a belle of the nineteenth century.*
MRS. BIGGS, *the Judge's guiding star.*

TIME. — *June, 1884.*

PLACE. — *Fort Lanark, N.M.*

Time of Representation, two hours and twenty minutes.

COSTUMES.

SEGURA. — *Acts I. and II.* — White flannel suit; wide-brim Mexican hat with gold cord; diamond ring and stud; long black mustache. *Act III.* — Uniform of Mexican general; blue coat, faced with red; gilt buttons; epaulets; dark blue trousers, slashed from knee to hem (outside seam), ornamented with rows of small gilt buttons; Mexican hat; sword-belt and sword; gloves; spurs.

LAWTON. — *Act I.* — Full-dress uniform, colonel U. S. A. *Acts II. and III.* — Fatigue dress; short, full beard, short hair, slightly gray.

WYBERT. — *Act I.* — Full-dress uniform, captain U. S. A. *Acts II. and III.* — Fatigue dress, with sword-belt and sword; light mustache.

BIGGS. — *Acts I. and II.* — Rusty black suit; soft hat; gray hair, partly bald; short, gray side whiskers. *Act III.* — Same costume, only soiled and torn.

CADWALLADER. — *Act II.* — Very "loud" imitation English travelling costume; plaid trousers; leggings; short coat; low-crown, double-visor cap; field-glass in case, slung over shoulder; walking-stick; single eyeglass; tiny pistol, cigarettes and matches in pocket. *Act III.* — Same as previous act, minus cap and all accessories; clothing torn; eye blackened. *Second dress,* ordinary walking suit.

BANGS. — *Acts II. and III.* — Exaggerated "cowboy" costume; rifle, knives, revolver.

CASEY. — *Acts I. and II.* — Uniform U. S. A. Chevrons of corporal on sleeves.

RETTA. — *Act I.* — Rich and elegant Spanish costume; short, quilted satin skirt; short jacket, trimmed with seguins; high, laced riding-boots; white mantilla; profusion of ornaments; dagger. *Act II.* — Similar dress, but of brighter colors. *Act III.* — Same as first act, with mantilla of black lace.

SOPHIA. — *Act I.* — Neat travelling costume. *Act II.* — House dress, appropriate for summer. *Act III.* — Light wrapper.

MAMIE. — *Act I.* — Rather "loud" tailor-made travelling dress. *Acts II. and III.* — House dress, slightly *outre.*

MRS. BIGGS. — *Acts I. II. and III.* — Quiet house dress.

PROPERTIES.

(See also " Costumes" and " Scene Plot.")

ACT I. — Bugles and drums to sound off L.; swords for LAWTON and PAUL; dagger for RETTA; stiletto for SEGURA.

ACT II. — Eyeglass, cigarettes, and matches, walking-stick, tiny pistol, and field-glass in case with shoulder-strap, for CADWALLADER; rifle, knives, and pistols for JOHNNIE; cigar, matches, and folded paper for SEGURA; swords for LAWTON and PAUL; bugles to sound and band to play off L.

ACT III. — Watch for MAMIE; rifle, etc., for JOHNNIE; band to play off L. U. E.; swords for SEGURA, PAUL, and LAWTON; folded paper for SEGURA; liquor flask and glass on table.

3

STAGE SETTINGS.
ACT I.

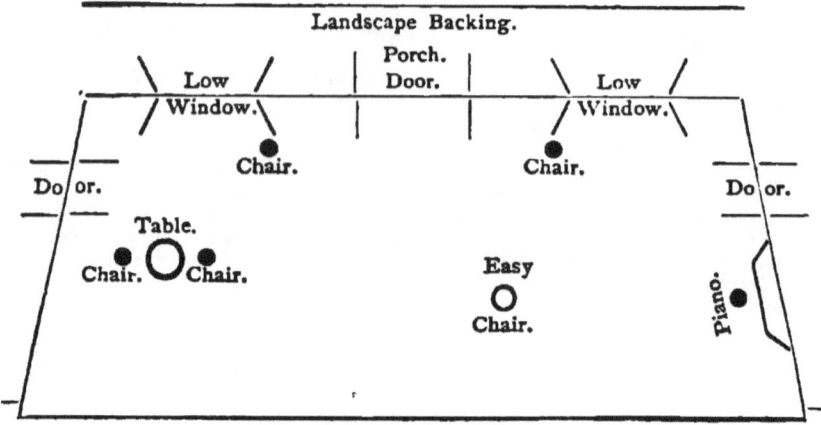

ACT II. *(See note below.)*

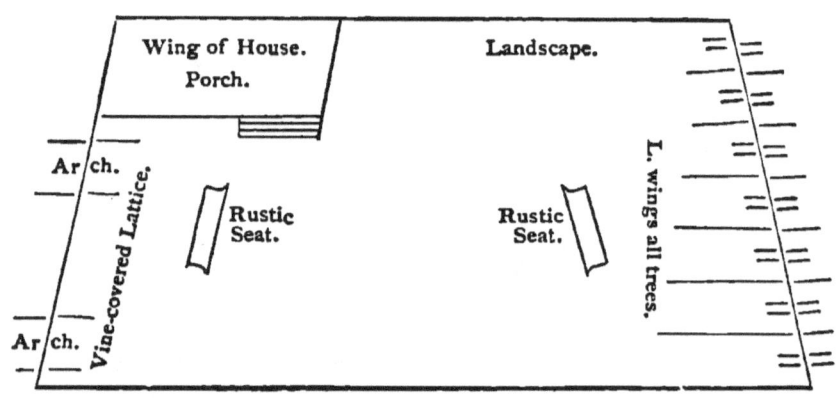

SCENE PLOT.

ACT I. — Sitting-room in LAWTON'S house in third grooves, with landscape and mountain backing in fifth grooves. Broad, low windows with draped curtains R. and L. in flat. Door C. in flat, opening on porch, also R. U. E. and L. U. E. Closed in. Ceiling. Piano L. Easy-chair L. C. Chairs near windows and beside table up R. Pictures on walls. Carpet and rugs.

ACT II. — Lawn in fifth grooves. Landscape on flat shows distant mountains. Bright sunlight effects. Sky border and sinks. House with practicable porch extends from R. U. E., one-third across stage. Balance of R. is a vine-covered lattice, with arches R. U. E. and R. I E. All L. wings are trees. Rustic seats R. and L.

ACT III. — Same as first act, except that curtains are drawn, and a lighted lamp is on table. Lights partly down. Landscape at first shows faint moonlight effects, which changes to early sunlight when curtains are draped back.

NOTE. — On a small stage, or where the scenery is limited, the second act may be played without change of scenery.

4

REMARKS ON THE PLAY.

This is a play of Western army life, but the army is only suggested. There are no battle scenes, Indians, horses, cowboys, nor red fire. The play is entirely domestic in treatment; and the exciting events which follow in rapid succession are rational effects from self-evident causes. The characters are well diversified, the action is brisk, and the interest is sustained until the last moment. In considering the relation of the characters to each other and to the story, the following suggestions by the author will be of interest.

SEGURA is a peculiar character, and should be studied with the utmost care. He is a man of wealth, education, and refined taste. He speaks pure English, with but the faintest possible accent. His bearing is easy, graceful, self-confident, and he appears to be a gentleman at all times, excepting when aroused by passion. And even then he should quickly recover his customary suave, polite manner. Avoid all melodramatic business, especially any glaring, stamping, hissing, or other stilted work. The cynical speeches should be given quietly, and with no appearance of studied effort. His age is about thirty-five, and the make-up is that of a Spaniard, — a trifle darker than usual, — with black hair, eyebrows and mustache. He speaks with quick, nervous energy, and his movements are energetic and forcible.

LAWTON is a man of fifty or thereabouts. He is quick and rather dogmatic in speech, usually exhibiting the bluff, positive manner of the successful military man. His face should be bronzed from exposure, and his hair and beard should be slightly gray.

WYBERT is the orthodox young lover. He is a high-spirited, quick-tempered man of twenty-five or thirty, and should be comparatively free from self-restraint in order to show up well in his interviews with SOPHIA and SEGURA. He wears a mustache and his face is slightly bronzed.

BIGGS is a man of fifty-five, stout, florid, partly bald, with short, gray side whiskers. His style is brisk, pompous, and grandiloquent. This is a comedy character throughout, and may be given considerable latitude. Deliver his long speeches *rapidly*, as the part will bear no dragging.

CADWALLADER must never be over-acted. The tendency indeed should be in the opposite direction, for to caricature this part is to ruin it. Immobility of countenance must be retained at all times, and the soft, effeminate style should be preserved until after his interview with MAMIE in the third act. His gestures should be few and stilted; and particular care should be taken to avoid overdoing the drawl in his speech. His age is about twenty-one.

BANGS. This character is simply that of a "fresh" young American, about seventeen years of age. Avoid overacting, especially when assuming the "tough." His speech should be rapid, his movements brisk and snappy.

CASEY is a typical stage Irishman, having nothing to particularly distinguish him from others of his class, except that, being a soldier, he must at all times assume an erect, military bearing.

RETTA is a difficult character to assume, and requires the most thorough and careful study to portray it with proper effect. She is called upon to represent such varying passions, — love, hate, joy, grief, anger, sorrow, jealousy, remorse, hope, fear, and the like, — that none but a careful, earnest actress should attempt the *rôle*. Petulance should be strictly avoided, together with all forced or unnatural emotion. It is very easy to overact a character of this sort ; and when that is done, the effect is grotesque. Quiet intensity is the most effective, and at no time should there be an attempt at high tragedy. The gestures should be few, and the voice should be pitched rather low than high. RETTA'S age is about sixteen, and her make-up should be that of an ideal Spanish girl, — a Castilian, dark, with black hair and eyebrows. The lady who assumes this part must needs look the character as well as act it.

SOPHIA should be played with much life, animation, and considerable freedom from restraint. Although the character is much lighter than RETTA'S, yet there should be a certain amount of dignified restraint underlying even her lightest moods, as she has considerable serious business, especially in her interviews with PAUL and SEGURA. Her age is nineteen years.

MAMIE is an *ingenue,* and therefore it is particularly necessary that she assume an air of unconscious innocence when delivering her somewhat "rapid" speeches. The least exhibition of self-consciousness destroys the illusion, and the character wearies instead of amusing. To be really effective, her words and actions must appear unstudied and free from all restraint. Age, about nineteen.

MRS. BIGGS is the characteristic "old woman." In this play she should be fat, fair, and — fifty. Her scene with MAMIE at the close of the second act is very effective, if well done, and very, *very* flat, if it is allowed to drag. Indeed, this character requires much vivacity in every scene, a fact which should be constantly borne in mind.

Particular attention must be given the music, which is an important factor, especially at the close of the second act. In the heavier scenes allow plenty of time for the necessary business, but keep the action brisk in the comic passages. The success of this play depends to a great extent upon the elaboration of the by-play and business ; therefore, especial care should be observed in casting the characters, and the play should never be presented without the most thorough and careful rehearsal.

SPECIAL NOTE. — The uniforms for LAWTON and WYBERT may be procured in any town having a military company or Grand Army Post. Elsewhere blue flannel suits will answer every purpose.

RIO GRANDE.

ACT I.

SCENE. — *Sitting-room at* LAWTON'S, *in 3d grooves. Door* C. *in flat opening on practicable porch. Doors,* R. U. E. *and* L. U. E. *Stage set as per* "*Scene Plot.*" *Discover* BIGGS *asleep in easy-chair,* L. C. *Bugles and drums sound of* L. U. E.

BIGGS (*sleepily*). Achoo! a-a-achoo! *achoo!* Shut the door! Confound you! shut — the — door! Why the devil — (*Yawns.*) Bless my soul, if I haven't been a — (*yawns*) sleep. Hanged if I couldn't sleep *thirty-six* hours a day without half trying. It's the a — (*yawns*) climate. That's what it is, the climate. (*Yawns.*)

(*Enter* MRS. BIGGS, R. U. E., *to* C.)

MRS. BIGGS. It's laziness, Mr. Biggs; that's what it is — laziness!

BIGGS. Mrs. Biggs!

MRS. B. Mr. Biggs!

BIGGS. Do you mean to stand there, as it were, Mrs. Biggs, under the high-arched dome of the Empyrean heavens, and assert that I — I — Judge Jeremiah Biggs, am slothfully sluggish?

MRS. B. Just so, Jerry. You know you are the laziest man on the Rio Grande.

BIGGS. Draw a line at th ˋ greasers, Mrs. Biggs; draw a line at the greasers, if you have any respect for my feelings.

MRS. B. Well, what are you loafing about here for?

BIGGS. Loafing, Mrs. Biggs? loafing? Understand me : I am here on business — particularly importantly pressing business.

MRS. B. Business! You? Ha, ha, ha! O Jerry! (*Goes* L. *laughing.*)

BIGGS. Mrs. Biggs (*she laughs*), Mrs. Biggs — I — you (*she laughs*) Mrs. *Biggs* — burr-r-r-r! (*Another laugh.*) Well, then, damn it, laugh — damn it, laugh! (*Crosses* R.)

MRS. B. There now, Jerry; don't lose your temper, Jerry. You would be in an awful pickle without it.

BIGGS. Mrs. Biggs, your hilarity is inconsequential, paradoxical, condemnationable, and I'll be everlastingly —

7

Mrs. B. Jeremiah Biggs!

Biggs. As it were. Ahem. To resume: The colonel, as you know, expects his daughter and several friends from the effete and decaying East to visit our untrammelled, free, and boundless West. They will arrive to-day. And I, as a representative citizen of this great and glorious country, consider it my paramount duty to receive them with hospitable arms, and show them the inconceivable wonders which await them.

Mrs. B. And get laughed at for your pains.

Biggs. Laugh at me — at me — me, Judge Biggs! You don't know what you're talking about. I'd fine 'em for contempt of court. Laugh at me! (*Crosses* L.)

Mrs. B. At all events, Miss Lawton will require none of your overpowering information.

Biggs. No, bless her heart! and if she did, I'd deputize Capt. Wybert.

Mrs. B. They're engaged, you know.

Biggs. No, I did *not* know, you know. By some occult demonstration a woman can locate an engagement anywhere between New York and San Francisco. Engaged, eh? And what will Señor Segura do when he hears of it?

Mrs. B. Who cares what he does? He's nothing but a Mexican.

Biggs. You're mistaken, my dear. Señor Segura is a Spanish-American, rich as mud, and proud as Lucifer. Still, I hope that your information regarding Capt. Wybert and Miss Sophia is correct. And I shall be most delightfully happy if, in my official capacity as magistrate, I am called upon to unite them in the beauteous bonds of holy matrimony. Here upon the classic banks of the far-famed Rio Grande; in this lovely land o'erflowing with milk and honey; with its gold, silver, copper, lead, iron, salt, Indians, greasers, and other rare and rank commodities (*exit* Mrs. Biggs, *disgusted*, R. U. E.) too somewhat numerous to mention; where the glowing golden sunlight falls across the opalescent-tinted mountains, those watchful sentinels of our limitless empire which throw their mystic shadows athwart the bounding river (*enter* Casey, C. D.), where men may come, and men may go, but I go on forever.

Casey. Then why the divil don't ye? By the piper that played before Moses, I belave ye air capable av it.

Biggs. Ah, corporal, I can't go on. I am —

Cas. Stuck? Ye don't mane it!

Biggs. With this glowing picture before me, words fail to express my emotion.

Cas. Shure that's jist what I thought 'tother day whin I kim down hard upon the business ind av a scorpion.

Biggs. You should never mind those trifling things.

Cas. Trifling? Shure it made me a lump as big as me two fists.

BIGGS. Your soul should be above the mere discomfort of a lump.

CAS. Aha, but the lump was not on me sowl at all, at all !

BIGGS. Good-by, corporal. I am going over to the railroad station where I shall await, with judicial calmness, the momentarily expected arrival of Miss Lawton and her most distinguished friends from the East. Therefore, *adios* (*at* C. D.). In the language of the poet, I must get me hence away. (*Exit* C. D.)

CAS. Now what the divil does he mane by gittin' his hins away ? Faith he kapes no hins at all excipt a few geese an' turkeys. He's a quare ould bird. I'm thinking he's mistooken his vocation. He ought to have been a phonograph — or else a mother-in-law.

(*Enter* LAWTON, C. D.)

LAWTON. Casey !

CAS. (*saluting*). Sor ?

LAW. Take a train wagon, with a couple of men, and drive over to the station for the baggage of the party.

CAS. Yis, sor. (*Salutes, going.*)

LAW. And, Casey —

CAS. (*saluting*). Yis, sor.

LAW. Be lively.

CAS. Yis, sor. (*Salutes, going.*)

LAW. And, Casey —

CAS. (*saluting*). Yis, sor.

LAW. A — that's all.

CAS. Yis, sor. (*Salutes, exit* C. D.)

LAW. And so my little girl is coming back again to her soldier father and soldier lover. I suppose we shall have that precious Segura hanging about here again. With all his wealth and ability I cordially dislike the fellow, and to —

(*Enter* SEGURA, C. D. *from* R.)

speak of the devil ! (*Goes* L.)

SEGURA. A thousand compliments, Col. Lawton, from your devoted servant.

LAW. (*stiffly*). Thank you, Señor Segura.

SEG. Has your beautiful and accomplished daughter arrived yet ? I was told that you expect her to-day.

LAW. My daughter has not yet arrived.

SEG. It will be such happiness to welcome her return. She, the life, the grace, the joy, of the garrison.

LAW. Thank you.

SEG. And I venture to hope that she will return whole-hearted ?

LAW. Indeed ! And I venture to hope that the question is her own affair. (*Crosses* R.)

SEG. (L.). Ah — the colonel will have his little joke. (*Aside*.) Damn the colonel!

LAW. You must excuse me, señor. I have some business requiring attention. Make yourself comfortable (*aside*) ; and be hanged to you! (*Exit* R. U. E.)

SEG. Thank you. (*Bows very low*.) The most comfortable thing I could do would be to run a knife under his fifth rib. I dislike him ; I detest the girl ; I hate the whole cursed American tribe ; but to get her in my power, — to crush the proud beauty as I crush my peons, — for that I would be fool enough to marry her. And the man who marries without just provocation, is the biggest fool possible.

(*Enter* RETTA, *quickly*, C. D. *from* L.)

RETTA. O uncle! I saw him, uncle! (*Looks off* L.) I saw him! He is here.

SEG. Who?

RET. Who? Why, Paul — Capt. Wybert. He doesn't know that we have arrived. Won't it be a surprise? Oh, I am so happy!

SEG. Bah! You simpleton! Have you no sense? If you want to lose your adorable captain altogether, just throw yourself at his head.

RET. I don't want to lose him! I don't (*stamping*)! I *won't* lose him! He shall love me — he *must* — or I will —

SEG. Finish your sentence ; or — you will kill him. Exactly. That is a part of woman's inheritance from Mother Eve.

RET. I — I would *not* harm him.

SEG. No? Not if he trampled on your heart — made it his plaything — cast off your love for another — flouted you — scorned you ? (RETTA *nervously clasps handle of dagger*.) Ah! I thought you would find that interesting.

RET. But he will not — he cannot forget that I saved his life after he was shot in that battle with the Indians.

SEG. Possibly not. But some day you will learn, my dear, that we men have short memories for past favors. Did this captain make love to you?

RET. No — not very much. I — I did about all the love-making.

SEG. Without doubt ; and therein you played the fool. Remember this fact : We "lords of creation" prefer to do the love-making and lying ourselves. (*Goes up* R.) When woman tries to woo she makes a mess of it, for she speaks the truth and — scares the game. (*Exit* R. U. E.)

RET. I wish I knew what he was talking about. It sounds very pretty and grand, but — oh, there he comes — there he comes! (*Retires up* L.)

(Enter PAUL, C. D., *from* L.)

PAUL *(down* C.). Sophia has arrived, and in about ten minutes I shall be the happiest fellow in New Mexico. Ten minutes? It's more like ten years. *(Sits.)* But I must not be impatient. Only I hope there won't be a crowd of the juniors tagging after. (RETTA *slips quietly behind him and covers his eyes with her hands.*) Hello! Oh, you rascal! I know who it is. I'll guess the first time. It is — it — is Sophia!

RET. *(indignantly)*. It is *not!* *(Crosses* R.)

PAUL *(rising)*. Retta! *(Aside.)* O Lord!

RET. Who is Sophia?

PAUL. Eh?

RET. *Who is Sophia?*

PAUL. Why — she is my — er — Miss Sophia Lawton.

RET. What is she to you?

PAUL. Eh?

RET. Um! *(Stamping.)* What — is — she — to you?

PAUL. She is — we are — er — I mean I am — *(Aside.)* Oh, hang it all!

RET. Well, sir!

PAUL. Look here, Retta! You have no right to question me in this manner, and you know it.

RET. Paul! Have you forgotten —

PAUL. No. I am profoundly grateful for your good services when I lay wounded at your home. I would gladly be your friend if I could. But — pardon me — mere friendship seems impossible with you.

RET. O Paul, Paul! I cannot believe it. *(Embracing him.)* Tell me you will — tell me —

PAUL. Good heavens, Retta! Can't you understand — don't you see —

(Enter LAWTON, C. D.)

LAW. Wybert — (RETTA *goes* L.)

PAUL *(saluting)*. Sir?

LAW. *(down* C.). Some scouts have brought in a report. I wish you would receive it.

PAUL. Yes, sir. *(Aside to* LAWTON.) For heaven's sake, get rid of her.

LAW. Who is she?

PAUL. Segura's niece; the beautiful devil who saved my life last summer.

LAW. Present me.

PAUL. Retta — allow me to present Col. Lawton; Colonel, the — the Señora Segura. I am called away on duty, so pray excuse me. *(Aside.)* Blessed relief! *(Exit* C. D. *to* R.)

LAW. When did you arrive, Miss Retta?

RET. A half-hour ago.

LAW. Then you came with your uncle?

RET. Yes. He had been here often, and this time I begged him to let me come. I wanted to see Paul, you know.

LAW. 'Hem — undoubtedly ; but I fear you will see very little of him. He is engaged —

RET. Engaged?

LAW. In military duties, you know. (*Aside.*) What a little fury !

RET. Military duties — oh, certainly. Capt. Wybert is a born soldier.

LAW. My daughter will be here directly, and I am sure that she will be delighted to welcome you as her guest, and to thank you for your Good Samaritan work with Capt. Wybert. (*Goes up* C.)

RET. So — then your daughter is —

LAW. (*at* C. D.). Here at last. (*Comes down* R.· RETTA *goes up* L.)

(*Enter* SOPHIA, *quickly,* C. D. *from* L.)

SOPH. (*running to* LAWTON). Oh, you dear, dear, darling old papa ! (*Embracing him.*) How glad I am ! How well you are looking ! Where is Paul ?

LAW. Receiving reports. He will be here directly. By the way, let me introduce you to Paul's good angel, who saved his life last summer. Señora Segura — may I have the pleasure — my daughter, Miss Lawton.

SOPH. (*crossing to her*). Who cannot thank you enough for your —

RET. Keep your thanks, if you please, until they are wanted ! (*Exit* R. U. E.)

SOPH. (*surprised*). Of all things ! And he called her an angel !

LAW. (*aside*). Whew ! I smell a rat. (*They go up* L.)

(*Enter* BIGGS *and* MAMIE, C. D *from* L.)

BIGGS. Ladies — ahem — ah — yes. This is the most beatific moment of my mundane, corporal existence. To welcome to the hospitable shores of the glorious Rio Grande the quintessence of youth and beauty, from the far-distant East — the American Orient, as it were ; to extend the right hand of joyful fellowship across the broad continent, bidding hail with stentorian lungs to the fair denizens of the sounding seaboard, and to clasp (*sees* MAMIE *calmly observing him*) — and to clasp, er — (*same business*) to clasp — er — ahem — (*same business*) yes, as it were.

MAMIE. Wind him up again ! He's run down !

BIGGS. Eh ?

MAM. Say, do you sell real estate ?

BIGGS. Real estate ? (*Aside.*) Bless my soul !

MAM. Because that's just the sort of comic opera a fellow gave the governor and me one day when we went to view a country-place in Jersey. My! He was a whole brass band, that fellow.

BIGGS. Was he mendacious — so to speak?

MAM. You mean was he a liar. Oh — no. He told the truth — great, big, square chunks of it. Said the soil was awfully wonderful — could raise anything. He was q. c. — quite correct. · The governor raised a mortgage the first thing; and Johnnie — that's my brother — he raised um — (*pointing downwards*) all summer long.

BIGGS (*aside*). I'm paralyzed. — Excuse me, please. I want to go away somewhere and think. Judge Biggs, you've met your match! O woman! O woman! O woman! (*Exit* R. U. E.)

MAM. Done up in a single round. Next.

SOPH. (*comes down with* LAWTON). Mamie — let me present my father, Col. Lawton; my friend, Miss Bangs.

LAW. I am very glad to meet you.

MAM. Thanks awfully. Who is that antique orator?

LAW. Judge Biggs — a capital old fellow, with a wonderful capacity for saying nothing. But where are the others?

MAM. Johnnie is getting his gun. He wants to shoot a few buffalo or Indians or tigers or something before dinner; and Mr. Cadwallader is back there helping your Irish corporal swear at the trunks.

LAW. Helping Casey?

MAM. Yes; Lieut. Cadwallader swears dreadfully. I have really known him to say, " Bah Jove."

LAW. (*half aside*). The devil!

MAM. No — the dude; but usually the lieutenant is very lady-like.

LAW. And so you had a military escort.

SOPH. Oh, yes; Lieut. Cadwallader is an N. G. soldier.

LAW. Eh?

MAM. N. G. S. N. Y. He is in the National Guard — the Dude's Own. (*Crosses to* LAWTON, L.)

(*Enter* PAUL, C. D.)

PAUL. Sophia!

SOPH. O Paul!

MAM. Go ahead. We won't look. (*Converses with* LAW-TON.)

PAUL. And you are really back again? (*They stand swinging hands.*)

SOPH. Really — really — really!

PAUL. Now I wonder if it *is* yourself.

MAM. Bite her and see.

PAUL. Thank you. (*Kisses* SOPHIA.)

MAM. Well?

PAUL. Genuine, I think. I'll make sure this time. (*Attempts to repeat kiss.*)

SOPH. Be-have! Let me present you. Mamie, allow me —

MAM. Oh, bother! It's Capt. Wybert and I'm Miss Bangs. Don't waste valuable time. (*Going.*)

SOPH. You need not go, Mamie.

MAM. Of course not. We wouldn't dream of it, would we, Colonel? (*Takes* LAWTON'S *arm and exits* R. U. E.)

PAUL. Rather rapid, isn't she?

SOPH. It is fashionable.

PAUL. Indeed? Then to be up to the times, a girl of *this* happy period must square her shoulders, talk horse, wear her brother's hat and coat, and shame the devil with slang.

SOPH. Oh, you cynic! And yet you pretend to love one of these dreadful creatures.

PAUL. But you are not fashionable.

SOPH. Oh, thank you!

PAUL. I mean in that way.

SOPH. No.

PAUL. Thank Heaven for it. Tell me about the others.

SOPH. Johnnie is her brother. There is Celtic blood in the family, and he has the most of it — mischief and all. He is a dreadful dime-novel desperado. Our other guest is Lieut. Cadwallader, a holiday soldier, whose knowledge of war is limited to a week once a year in the State encampment, and a weekly drill at the armory. They are very anxious to kill a few Indians

PAUL. And they will have a chance.

SOPH. A chance? Surely — O Paul, you don't expect trouble?

PAUL. At any moment. The authorities at Washington, according to custom, have fed, clothed, and petted the red devils all winter; and now that summer is here we may expect an outbreak at any point.

SOPH. But not here?

PAUL. Very likely. I have received a report from our scouts, and they tell me trouble is brewing.

SOPH. (*half crying*). Then you will go and get shot again, and that horrid Spanish girl —

PAUL. Tut, tut; she saved my life, remember.

SOPH. And now she claims it, too. Oh, I saw the demon of jealous hatred in her eyes when I tried to thank her. (*Crosses* R.)

PAUL (*aside*). There will be an awful row.

SOPH. I suppose it is very flattering to you.

PAUL. Now, my darling, don't *you* be jealous.

SOPH. Well — who has a better right?

PAUL. Nobody of course. But come now, don't make us both unhappy over nothing.

SOPH. Is *she* nothing?

PAUL. To me? Yes.

SOPH. But don't you admire her? Be careful now!

PAUL. I admire her pluck. When my horse went down in that mad charge, and I lay wounded and helpless at the mercy of an ambushed gang of Apaches, it was she alone who rode like a whirlwind into the crowd and whipped them single handed. Isn't that something to admire?

SOPH. (*doubtfully*). Ye—yes. But you won't fall in love with her because of that?

PAUL. No.

SOPH. Never, never, never?

PAUL. Never — never — never.

SOPH. Then you may —

PAUL. Seal the compact? I will. (*Kisses her.*)

(*Enter* SEGURA, R. U. E., *comes down* C.)

PAUL. There — the sky is clear again.

SEG. My compliments to Miss Lawton.

SOPH. Oh, Señor! (*Crosses* L.)

PAUL (*aside*). Confound the Señor!

SEG. Are we to have amateur theatricals at the garrison?

SOPH. Amateur theatricals?

SEG. And perhaps I interrupted a rehearsal.

PAUL. Sir, do you —

SEG. Don't be offended. These little comedies are so very amusing. Of course if it were possible to be serious upon such an occasion, the result might be disastrous — at least to some. (SOPHIA *goes up* L.)

PAUL. What do you mean, sir? Do you infer —

SEG. Nothing whatever. To a man like you, inference is quite unnecessary.

PAUL. What in the devil are you driving at?

SEG. Bah! A blind man should see.

PAUL. Perhaps you want a quarrel.

SEG. Really?

PAUL (*hotly*). If you do, sir, you will find me —

SEG. Don't exert yourself. I only quarrel with *gentlemen.*

PAUL. You've gone too far, sir. I've a mind —

SEG. You forget. There is a lady present. If you want satisfaction, I shall be most happy to furnish it, when and where you choose.

PAUL. And you may be sure I will! (*They go up* R. *and* C.)

(*Enter* MAMIE, *quickly*, C. D.)

MAM. Oh, I'm dead! I'm dead! I know I am!

SOPH. (*beside her*). Poor child! What killed you?

MAM. You needn't laugh at me, so now!

PAUL (L.). But what was it?

MAM. A great, horrid, awful, terrible alligator!

ALL. What!

MAM. I don't care. It was an alligator or — or something. And it jumped right at my stock— er — ahem ! — Well, you know.

PAUL. It was the — ha, ha, ha ! (*Goes up* L., *laughing.*)

MAM. Oh, was it ? Well, I'm glad I've found out — awfully !

SOPH. It belongs to the Judge. Don't be frightened. Doubtless he thought you were a — a — (*turns away, laughing*) ha, ha, ha !

MAM. If the Judge thinks I'm a "ha, ha, ha," I'll break my parasol over his head !

(*Enter* CASEY, C. D.)

MAM. Corporal, did you see him ?

CAS. (*saluting*). Indade I did ; an' who is he ?

MAM. That dreadful monster ?

SOPH. The Judge's pet.

CAS. Ye mane the lizard. Shure. I did, Miss, an' it threw me into a state av temporary insanity, so it did. (*Aside to* PAUL.) The Colonel is axin' fur ye, sor ; more scouts have arrived, and the divil an' all is to pay. An' av ye plaze, sor, he sez kape mum.

PAUL. All right. (CASEY *salutes and exit* C. D.)

MAM. (*glancing at* SEGURA). Who is the mysterious stranger ?

PAUL. A — Spanish-American.

MAM. Gentleman or "gent"?

PAUL. Neither.

MAM. Stupendous ! Present him.

PAUL. Excuse me. (*Bows and exit* C. D.)

MAM. (*aside*). Um — case of green-eyed monster ; dark green, too ; b-a-d case.

SOPH. Come, Mamie, let me show you my cabinet of minerals.

SEG. (*down* C.). Pardon me, ladies ; but will Miss Lawton favor me with a brief interview — in private?

SOPH. (*aside*). Oh, dear !

MAM. (*aside*). Another victim ! Oh, my — gimini ! (*Exit* R. U. E.)

SEG. Be seated, pray. (*They sit* L.) What I desire to say, Miss Lawton, has been in my mind for a long time. I should have spoken before this ; but you will readily understand that a man of my rank and station in life cannot permit himself to be hasty in judgment. Therefore, as the subject which I am about to present — have I the honor of your attention? — thank you ; as the subject is one of vital importance, it has been well considered, in all its bearings ! My estates beyond the Rio Grande, as you may know, are princely in extent. with mines which yield a royal ransom every year. My flocks and herds are countless, and unnumbered peons are mine to command. All this, with heart and hand, I lay at your feet. I await your answer.

SOPH. Señor Segura, you honor me too much ; I — I am —

SEG. Not at all. It is I who will be honored. Have I then permission to address your father ?

SOPH. Believe me, Señor, I appreciate your offer, but — (*rising*) it would be useless.

SEG. Useless — indeed? (*Rising.*) May I venture to ask the reason?

SOPH. Because — I —

SEG. Go on, please. Because? —

SOPH. Frankly, then, I do not love you.

SEG. That is wholly unnecessary.

SOPH. Señor!

SEG. Certainly. I am quite in earnest, I assure you. Love is all very well in the abstract, but it borders too closely on hate for comfort. Esteem and regard are much pleasanter. And assuredly you respect me — do you not?

SOPH. Yes — but respect without love —

SEG. Is all I ask.

SOPH. Then seek a woman who will wed you on those terms. If I loved you, which I do not; if I were free to wed you — which I am not — I would never disgrace my American birth by giving my hand in such contemptible barter. (*Crosses* R.)

SEG. An excellent doctrine. What a pity it is that your title-hunting American sisters do not oftener observe it!

SOPH. That sneer is unworthy of you, Señor. (*Going.*)

SEG. (*stopping her*). Pardon me. If I heard rightly, you intimated that your hand is already pledged. I take it for granted then that the little comedy I witnessed between you and your upstart Captain was a beautiful and romantic scene from real life — on your own part, at least.

SOPH. You grow insulting, sir. Let me pass.

SEG. Answer me this —

(*Enter* PAUL, *quickly*, C. D.)

PAUL. Answer him nothing!

SEG. How, sir!

SOPH. Paul, I entreat you —

PAUL. One moment. (*Enter* RETTA, R. U. E., *remaining quietly at back.*) This lady will answer no questions from you. (SOPHIA *goes to* L. C.)

SEG. Astonishing! And why not?

PAUL (*hotly*). Because she is a lady; because she is my affianced wife, and as such will hold no communication with a greaser like you! (*Exit with* SOPHIA, L. U. E. *As he turns away,* SEGURA *with a muttered curse draws knife and is about to follow, when* RETTA *throws herself in front of him, clasping her arms around his neck.*)

RET. No, no, no!

SEG. (*striving to break loose*). Stand aside! I tell you — stand aside!

RET. What would you do?

SEG. (*savagely*). And what would you do?

RET. Nothing.

SEG. Ay, but you would. You would have me spare the life of that upstart beggar who has crossed my path, scorned your love, and broken your heart. (*Crosses* L.)

RET. Perhaps he — he will yet remember —

SEG. Humph! Are you such a fool as that?

RET. But I — oh, I cannot bear it — I cannot bear it. (*Drops into chair by table.*)

SEG. And are you so weak — you in whose heart beats the proudest blood of old Castile? Then pity him, weep for him, pray for him, while he laughs and jeers at your misery!

RET. Oh!

SEG. And perhaps your rival —

RET. (*quickly*). My rival!

SEG. Yes, your rival — your scornful, doll-faced rival — will laugh with him. Oh, it will be rare sport!

RET. (*springing up*). Tell me, tell me what I can do.

SEG. Ah, you are touched at last!

RET. Plan, contrive, conjure up something, anything, however devilish, which shall make *her* feel the agony that I endure.

SEG. Kneel, then, and repeat my words. (*She kneels* C.) " I swear by the Blessed Mother — that while life remains — I will stop at nothing — until my wrongs are righted." (*She repeats.*) There! (*Draws her to him.*) Now you are, indeed, worthy of the land that gave you birth!

QUICK CURTAIN.

ACT II.

SCENE. — *Lawn in* 5*th grooves; entrances* L., *through tree wings and through arches,* R. U. E. *and* R. I E. *Practicable porch to set house* R. W. E ; *rustic seats* R. *and* L.

(*Enter* MAMIE *and* CADWALLADER, L. U. E.)

MAM. There — it's over with.

CADWALLADER. Ya-as. And I'm awfully glad.

MAM. Wasn't the drilling perfectly splendid?

CAD. Well, I cawn't say that it was. Some of the men looked fike vawy common fellahs, and I don't like the cut of their uniforms at all, don't you know. I don't like men whose clothes don't fit.

MAM. But I thought they got there in their evo-what-do-you-call-ems in great shape.

CAD. Oh, ya-as — they *did* do vawy well foh ordinary *pwofessional* soldiers, don't you know, but of cawse they cawn't compaw with *our* wegiment.

MAM. And, besides, they haven't any officers like you.

CAD. No, indeed, they haven't. Fellahs who follow a militawy twade foh *pay*, cawn't expect to equal gentlemen who dwill foh pastime.

MAM. Of course not. (*Aside.*) Oh, isn't he a delicious guy?

CAD. And then this dweadful out-of-the-way place must wuin all the finah feelings. No cigawettes, no soda watah, no vapoh baths, no stage doahs, no kettledwums, —

MAM. And sometimes the soldiers really *do* have to fight!

CAD. Isn't it dweadful! Think of soldiers fighting! My wegiment *nevah* does anything like that! But I suppose it's all wight enough foh these common soldiers.

MAM. It's lucky that you are no common soldier.

CAD. Ya-as.

MAM. Now, if there *should* be war, I know that Col. Lawton will ask your advice.

CAD. (*complacently*). No doubt.

MAM. And you will give it, won't you, lieutenant?

CAD. Ya-as, of cawse.

MAM. And go off and get killed for glory?

CAD. (*doubtfully*). Ye-ya-as; but — aw (*nervously, without drawl*), I say, Miss Bangs, you — you don't suppose that there *will* be trouble?

MAM. Oh, no. (*Aside, highly amused.*) He's talking United States, by all that's wonderful! (*Aloud.*) No, there will be no trouble, but there may be some red-hot fighting; so you better get your hair cut right off short.

CAD. Why had I?

MAM. So they can't scalp you.

CAD. This is dreadful. I (*with an effort*) aw — I mean *dweadful.* Excuse me, Miss Bangs, I have some business to look aftah. (*Aside.*) I'll wun wight down and see when the next twain leaves foh home. (*Exit* L. I E.)

MAM. If I can only scare a little manhood into him, and a big lot of the dude out, he will make a very decent fellow. (*Commotion off* R. U. E.) Hello! There's a row, and Johnnie is into it up to his neck.

(*Enter* JOHNNIE, CASEY, *and* BIGGS, R. U. E.)

CAS. Luk here, young feller; ye jist bate the divil out o' sight, so ye do.

BIGGS. He is certainly a most remarkably incorrigible specimen of purely unadulterated youthful depravity.

JOHNNIE. Set 'em up again! When *did* you swallow that dictionary?

MAM. Jonathan Montgomery Bangs!

JOHN. Keno! Go to the head!

MAM. You dreadful boy! What *have* you been doing?

CAS. 'Doin', is it? Shure, miss, he jist was afther shootin' ther Jedge's cow full o' holes — bad cess to him!

JOHN. I thought she was a buffalo.

MAM.   John Montgome —

JOHN.   Oh, skip it! I don't care. Why didn't he put a label on his blamed old milk tank.

MAM.   Send your bill to papa.

JOHN.   Along with the cow, and the compliments of J. Montgomery Bangs.

CAS.   Faith, I wish he belonged to me fer jist wan minute. I'd bang him!

JOHN. (*swaggering*). Whatter ye soy? If you want blood, call on me. I'm the *baddest* kind of a bad man, and I live on nails and gunpowder.

MAM.   You will live on bread and water if you don't behave, for I'll have the colonel lock you up.

JOHN.   Not muchly now. I'm the colonel's right bower, I am. See? There's going to be war, sis, an' I'm all there. I shall return from this campaign covered all over with scalps and glory. That's my gait. Come along, Mame. There's Miss Sophia looking for us. Perhaps she sees an Injun. Woh! (*Follows* MAMIE *off* L. I E.)

CAS.   Say, judge, now what do ye suppose the loikes o' him was iver made for onyhow?

BIGGS.   Your problem, corporal, is one that has taxed the ingenuity of the greatest writers, thinkers, and psychological students —

CAS. (*aside*). O Lord!

BIGGS (*continuing*). Since the dawn of American history. His mother doubtless imagines that he was created to be President of the United States, in which idea she has a monopoly, since most people know that he was born to be hung. Hem! Now the American small boy — even when he sheds his knickerbockers — is *sui generis;* he certainly is not *pro bono publico.* Ahem! (CASEY *quietly exits* R. U. E.) In the actual point of fact, the earlier writers on anthropology strenuously insist that this disproportionableness is *prima facie* evidence that (*looks around*) that — that, oh, damn it! (*Goes up* C.) It is a strange fact that whenever I open the storehouses of my wisdom, Mrs. Biggs goes to sleep, and everybody else goes away.

(*Enter* CADWALLADER, L. U. E.)

CAD.   Oh, deah! I might have known I'd get into twouble!

BIGGS.   What is the matter?

CAD.   Why, they say the wed skins have pulled up the twack so the twains cawn't wun, and that I cawn't possibly get away.

BIGGS.   And, sir, may I ask, why do you *want* to get away — to leave this grand and glorious country, this favored land of milk and honey — where the golden sunshine mantles the brow of the towering Magdalena Mountains, —

CAD.   Oh, *blawst* the Magdalena Mountains!

BIGGS.   Sir!

CAD. And blawst the blawsted country!

BIGGS. Sir! I — damn it, sir; that talk is felonious felony! It's double-dyed treason, sir — treason!

CAD. Do you suppose I want to go fighting those dweadful, dirty, ill-smelling Indians, with their wags and tatters?

BIGGS. Ah!

CAD. I don't mind a *sham* battle on the pawade gwound, don't you know, because there is always a cwowd of ladies awound, don't you know, and a fellah can go home and take a bath when it is ovah, and have his valet bwush him up. (*Crosses* R.)

BIGGS (L.). Yah! I'm getting sick!

(*Enter* SEGURA, R. U. E.)

SEG. Good-morning, lieutenant. Good-morning, judge. Why, *Santa Maria!* You look as if you had taken something disagreeable.

BIGGS. So I have: a dose of American — yah — "aristocracy!"

SEG. (*glancing at* CAD.). I understand. It is a regular blue pill!

CAD. I say, Mr. Segura, about these blawsted Indians; do you think there is weally any — aw — that is — you see —

SEG. Danger? For you? None whatever. The Indian is a peculiar animal; he never harms people who are *non compos mentis.*

BIGGS. Then *he* is safe.

CAD. Thanks awfully. (*Aside.*) Now, what the dooce is *non compos mentis?* Blawst his Spanish lingo!

SEG. I should imagine, lieutenant, being a military man, that you would delight in a campaign.

CAD. Ya-as — I suppose it *is* more exciting than lawn tennis. But, then, one is likely to get so fwightfully soiled and dirty — and the guns make such a wacket — and you have to dwink out of nasty tin cups, and all that, don't you know. This, of cawse, to one of the awistocwacy —

SEG. Aristocracy?

CAD. Ya-as.

SEG. By the way, what *is* an American aristocrat?

CAD. The dooce! Why, any ignowamus could answer that.

SEG. I am all attention. Proceed.

CAD. It's a fellah of — of the uppah clawss — who has — aw — plenty of money — belongs to the clubs — has a valet to look aftah him and dwess him — who dwinks plain soda — aw — and nevah associates with common people; who — who — gets his clothes from London, and — aw —

SEG. Whose grandfather ran a gin mill, sold furs, or raised cabbages! And who, therefore, looks down with sublime contempt on all honest labor; who is too weak to argue, too cowardly to resist, and too contemptible to kick! (*Crosses* L.)

CAD. Look heah. Now — I — I —

BIGGS. 'Sh! Be careful —

CAD. But I cawn't stand that, and I won't. I'll —

BIGGS. Dry up! Unless you want to be an angel!

CAD. Eh?

BIGGS. That man can snuff a candle at twenty paces, and **he is** the devil himself with a knife.

CAD. (*frightenea*). The dooce! Say — (*They converse aside.*)

(*Enter* LAWTON, R. U. E.)

LAW. Señor Segura — a word, please.

SEG. With pleasure. (*Goes up.*)

CAD. I wonder if I should offah to tweat him to a cigawette —

BIGGS. Then he'd kill you anyhow — vivisect you — skin **you** alive. Come along! (*Exit, with* CAD. R. I E.)

SEG. So you think the outbreak will be serious?

LAW. I fear so.

SEG. And you intend to crush them out this time?

LAW. I certainly do — provided they make a stand of it, and —

SEG. And the "old women" at Washington don't interfere.

LAW. Exactly.

SEG. Very well. I will order out a force of cavalry on our side of the river, to cut off retreat; and, if you choose, I will instruct my men to co-operate with you, — or perhaps will lead them in person.

LAW. A thousand thanks, señor.

SEG. You are quite welcome, colonel.

(*Enter* CASEY, R. U. E. *Salutes* LAWTON.)

LAW. What is it?

CAS. (*saluting*). The scouts are in, sor, an' waitin' to report, sor.

LAW. I will see them directly. (CASEY *salutes and exits*, R. U. E.) Will you join me, señor?

SEG. In a few moments. I must despatch a courier with orders.

LAW. Very well. (*Aside.*) He's a very decent fellow after all. (*Exit* R. U. E.)

SEG. He is a bigger fool than I thought. Oh, yes — yes. My men will co-operate with him! Precisely. (*Lights cigar.*) Just as the Prussians did with Napoleon in Russia. Allies are never reliable, and I shall be surprised if my men fail to do some very — careless — shooting. If this cursed Wybert is killed — well and good; it will save me the trouble. If he escapes — so much the worse — for him.

(*Enter* RETTA, R. U. E.)

RET. Uncle!

SEG. Well, my dear? (*Seated* L.)

RET. Are you doing nothing?

SEG. I am doing something.

RET. (*impatiently*). Well, what?

SEG. (*coolly*). Smoking.

RET. You have lost heart. You mean to spare them.

SEG. Indeed? You surprise me.

RET. Do I? And you surprise me — you, whose path no one has ever crossed in safety ; whom the natives call " the lightning " because of your deadly skill — and before whom the fiercest bandit slinks and crawls with fear.

SEG. (*removing hat*). My dear Retta — you flatter me !

RET. Yes? Then does it flatter you to say that I am disgusted with your indifference — that I really believe you dare not —

SEG. Stop where you are. *I* dare not? What do you mean ?

RET. You seem so quiet that I — I —

SEG. (*rising*). My dear, did you ever observe a storm coming out from the West? Have you watched the gray clouds rising slowly to the zenith, while the air grew heavy, and Nature's voice was hushed in fear? Have you thought that amid that strange and awful silence the deadly thunderbolts were being forged? And when at last the fierce lightning sprang forth, was it not all the more terrible for the long silence? Answer me.

RET. Yes.

SEG. Good. I have stored the lightning.

RET. Well ?

SEG. And it will strike —

RET. (*eagerly*). Yes —

SEG. When I see fit. (*As* RETTA *turns away.*) Here — sign this paper. (*Takes paper from pocket.*)

RET. What is it ?

SEG. *Your — marriage — certificate !*

RET. (*hesitating, in doubt*). My — marriage — certificate ?

SEG. You heard me. That paper certifies to your marriage with Paul Wybert.

RET. But I am not — this paper is a — a —

SEG. Forgery? It is quite possible. My skill with the pen is something remarkable.

RET. This is madness ! We shall be exposed.

SEG. My dear child, I am not *quite* a fool ! Observe me. The priest is dead whose excellent name I have — well — borrowed for this occasion. The witnesses are my creatures who would swear away their souls' salvation to spite an American.

RET. If they should not —

SEG. Then I would cut their throats.

RET. But the marriage register ?

SEG. Will quietly disappear.

RET. Your plan is fiendish.

SEG. As I intended.

RET. I'll not do it.

SEG. What ? Be careful, now !

RET. I cannot — I cannot !

Seg. Very well. Then your lovely rival wins him. She will flaunt her victory before your eyes, while people will utter covert sneers, and openly point to you as the cast-off toy of the American!

Ret. Uncle! You torture me. (*Crosses* R.)

Seg. Look yonder! (*Pointing* L.) There they go. See how she smiles on him — and how happy he is. Now they look this way. See — they are laughing at you. Isn't it delightful? Ah, Señora. How you *must* enjoy it!

Ret. Give me the paper — quick — give it me! Where shall I sign?

Seg. There — under his name.

Ret. Yes — I can see her wither and shrink before this. I can see her proud head droop, and the haughty light fade from her eyes. Ah, I could cry for joy — I am so happy! Wait for me. I will return in a moment. (*Exit* R. U. E.)

Seg. How easy it is to make a fool of her. A passionate woman is the most unaccountable creature on earth, for she loves or hates without rhyme or reason. Touch her heart and she will blow hot or cold — kill or caress — all in a single breath.

(*Enter* Retta, *quickly*, R. U. E.)

Ret. I have signed the paper.

Seg. 'Sh! Don't tell all creation.

Ret. Do you want it?

Seg. Yes. (*Takes paper.*) Say nothing of this.

Ret. I am on fire with impatience.

Seg. No doubt of it.

Ret. I want to see her fall at my feet, crushed and broken; to see her weep her heart out in bitter agony as I have done. I cannot wait for the time. Do hurry! (*Crosses* L.)

Seg. My dear, your true epicure does not bolt his food nor pour down his imperial Tokay; and only a fool kills an enemy quickly, if he can place the soul itself upon the rack.

Ret. Oh, what a splendid hater!

Seg. For I study it. Hating is an art which should never be governed by passion. Yesterday I only *disliked* this Capt. Wybert, and would have killed him with pleasure; to-day I cordially *hate* him, and would not harm his precious *body* for the world.

Ret. What would you do?

Seg. Ruin him — disgrace him — scourge him from the sight of honest men; make his life a waking nightmare — an *inferno* — surpassing even Dante's wildest dream.

Ret. But his "dear Sophia" — what of her?

Seg. That is your part in our little drama. You must arouse her jealousy — set them to quarrelling — and thus stir up the devil all around. When you meet Wybert you must act submissive — chastened; thus you disarm suspicion and gain his confidence.

Then awaken pity by your tears and self-reproaches. Tell him you are unworthy —

RET. Uncle!

SEG. It is a lie, of course; but all is fair in love and war. Besides, it will be an amusing turnabout, for man has lied to woman since the dawn of history. (*Exit* R. I E.)

RET. Not worthy of him? No — and can never be. Paul is noble, grand, honorable — while I am a base, sinful girl. Can I sink so low that I may chide myself thus? No! I will not! (*Goes up* C.) I will have no share in such a monstrous crime. I will — (*looks* L.) oh — there they are! He is bidding her good-by — his arm is around her — their lips meet — I — I — O God, my heart is breaking! (*Sinks into seat*, R., *sobbing; a pause; then looks up with fierce, sudden joy.*) He said I must act submissive, chastened. Yes! And thus divert suspicion! I can! I will! He shall applaud me as an actress! Yes! (*goes up.*) Here comes Paul — my audience! Ah, how I hate him — how I hate him! (*Sits* R.)

(*Enter* PAUL, L. U. E.)

PAUL. The government ought to be — blessed. Thanks to the old grannies at Washington we are called upon to feed the cursed Indians all winter and fight them all summer. I rather enjoy a row myself, but just at the present moment I feel like (*sees* RETTA) the um-m!

RET. Paul — Capt. Wybert — I — wish to speak with you for a moment.

PAUL. Yes — I know; I am very sorry, but I really have no time to spare. (*Going.*)

RET. Paul —

PAUL. Well?

RET. Not a moment in all eternity?

PAUL. What do you mean?

RET. That you will never see me again; that I shall annoy you no more. If I feel no shame when I confess that I have loved you with all my heart and soul, it is because I know how hopeless and unvalued that love is. Perhaps you will think me bold, unmaidenly —

PAUL. Why, Retta —

RET. But forgive me, Paul, and pity me. I should have known that you could never, never love one so unworthy as I — I — (*sobbing.*)

PAUL. Unworthy? Retta, child, don't debase yourself by such words. You make me feel like a hard, insensible brute. It is I who am unworthy of such love as yours — I whose very life should be yours to command. If I had known —

RET. Stop! You cannot undo the past. You are bound to another, and must not think of me until — until I am gone!

PAUL. But, Retta —

RET. You will not think of me harshly when I am dead — will you, Paul? You will sometimes let your memory linger kindly upon the poor girl, untutored in the ways of the world, who would gladly have given up her life for you, and whose dying breath was an orison for your happiness.

PAUL (*much affected*). Don't, Retta. Your words unman me. (*Sits L.*)

RET. (*aside*). I wonder how I am doing? (*Goes up slightly and looks L.*) And *she* is watching us! Excellent — excellent! Now for it! (*Comes down and kneels beside* PAUL.) And you, too, are going away. In this world we may never meet again. Do you forgive me?

· PAUL. I have nothing to forgive.

RET. Then will you promise me something?

PAUL. What is it?

RET. Promise that you will tell no living soul what passed in this interview.

PAUL. I promise.

RET. And will you grant me one more favor — only one?

PAUL. Gladly.

RET. Then put your arms around me, and kiss me, Paul, for the first and last time. (*He does so.*) Thank you. (*They rise.*) I am faint and weary. Please take me in. (*They go* R., *and* RETTA *draws his arm around her.*)

(*Enter* SEGURA *and* SOPHIA, L. U. E. *He restrains her.*)

RET. I can trust you, then?

PAUL (*puzzled*). Trust me? Why, yes — certainly you can.

RET. Ah, Paul, now I can bid you good-by with resignation, for you have taken such a load from my heart. (*They exit*, R. I E.)

SOPH. You saw that?

SEG. With lasting regret.

SOPH. Oh, indeed!

SEG. Believe me — truly. Capt. Wybert was my guest some months ago, and pretended to conceive a great passion for my niece — whose guardian I am. Although I strongly opposed his suit, yet I considered him a man of honor. Certainly I never dreamed that he was engaged to you. This, I trust, will excuse my apparent ill-temper of last evening.

SOPH. Yes. I — I appreciate your motive. But your niece should be told —

SEG. She has been.

SOPH. And yet —

SEG. She hinted at something more than a mere engagement.

SOPH. Something more? Can it be possible that —

SEG. My niece is an honest girl, Miss Lawton, however head-strong and wilful.

SOPH. Then it is I whom that profligate would have duped! Oh, the shame, the humiliation, of this moment!

SEG. Poor child ! I pity you.

SOPH. Señor Segura, yesterday you professed regard for me.

SEG. Yes —

SOPH. To-day, if you can take me as I am, with a heart of ashes, shamed, degraded, in my own eyes — then — I am yours.

SEG. (*embracing her*). Mine, at last !

(*Enter* PAUL, *quickly*, R. U. E.)

PAUL. Sophia !

SEG. Well, sir, what is it ?

PAUL (*hotly*). Unhand that lady !

SEG. (*sneering*). How very melodramatic !

PAUL. By Heaven, I'll —

SEG. (*facing him with folded arms*). Will you ?

SOPH. Señor — please — leave me for a moment.

SEG. Your servant. (*Kisses her hand, and exits*, L. U. E.)

SOPH. Well, sir ?

PAUL. Tell me what this means.

SOPH. Do you wish to know ? Then look into your own false heart for the answer.

PAUL. Are you mad ?

SOPH. Yes ; mad with rage at your duplicity.

PAUL. *My* duplicity ? Well — I'll be hanged !

SOPH. No doubt of it.

PAUL. My duplicity ! Mine ? And perhaps *you* will explain —

SOPH. Yes, when *you* explain the meaning of the scene which I have witnessed.

PAUL. Oh, that ! Why, you see — (*Aside.*) Devil take the luck ! I promised to say nothing. You — er — you see —

SOPH. Precisely ; I did see, — to your shame be it said.

PAUL. But, my dear —

SOPH. That will do. Don't add another falsehood to your infamy.

PAUL. Sophia ! You will regret this.

SOPH. No. I can only regret the day when first I met you. (*Crosses* R. PAUL *goes up* C. *Bugles sound off* L. U. E.)

PAUL. What you saw bears no disgrace to me. *I* cannot, in honor, explain ; but, will *you* not? (*A pause.*) Very well then. The assembly is called. My command is waiting. I shall soon go out to battle, and if I never return — O Sophia, tell me — shall we part like this ? I will forget what I witnessed ; I will believe nothing ill of you. Can you not return faith for faith ?

SOPH. Tell me what you were saying.

PAUL. I can tell you nothing.

SOPH. Then go ! (*Sits* R.)

PAUL So be it. (*Martial music sounds faintly*, L. U. E.) I had thought of this campaign with pride, if not with joy ; for it promised me new honors and higher rank, which should all be yours. Now, I think of nothing but the death I court; for 1 know that if my life goes out it will cause you neither pain nor sorrow. Farewell, then, Sophia. Farewell. God bless you. (*Exit quickly*, L. U. E. *Music dies away. Brief pause.*)

SOPH. (*startled*). Paul! (*Rising.*) Paul! (*Up* L.) Gone! Gone! Oh, my heart! (*Sobs.*)

(*Enter* LAWTON, R. U. E.)

LAW. (*briskly*). Well, my dear, we're off.

SOPH. (*embracing him*). Father!

LAW. There, there. It may be nothing but a skirmish, and perhaps they won't even show fight.

SOPH. Then why go at all?

LAW. Come, come, my dear! Remember, you are a soldier's daughter. Remember, too, that if anything happens to me, there is a Father above (*cap off—solemnly*) whose loving eye will watch over you by day and by night; whose loving hand will guide and protect you forever. (*Music as before.*) There, the boys are waiting for me. Good-by, my dear child. (*Kisses her.*) Good-by. (*Exit*, L. U. E.)

SOPH. (*brokenly*). Good-by. (*Follows to* L. U. E. *Stands looking off. Music fainter.*)

(*Enter* MR. *and* MRS. BIGGS, R. U. E.)

BIGGS. Mrs. Biggs, your remarks, as usual, are highly edifying; nevertheless, however, I am under the necessity of saying *au revoir*.

MRS. B. Have you got that dreadful what-do-you-call-it again?

BIGGS. No, my dear; "*au revoir*" is *not* the toothache. It means, in simple English, farewell for the present particular time being until another day's bright sunshine gilds the knell of parting day, and all that sort of thing; you understand?

MRS. B. Yes; but what *are* you talking about?

BIGGS. Well, Mrs. Biggs, the regiment is going off hunting Indians —

MRS. B. And you are gug-gug-going, too, Jeremiah?

BIGGS. Such is my present, duly considered, unchangeable resolution.

MRS. B. Don't go and leave me a widow, Jeremiah. (*Embracing him.*) Say you won't, you darling old Jerry. (*He shakes his head.*) You precious old fool!

BIGGS. Eh! What! Damme! I'll fine you for contempt of court!

MRS. B. Fine your great-grandmother's fourth cousin!

BIGGS. 'Sh-sh! Keep mum! I'm going out with Lieut. Cadwallader. He has paid me to conduct him to a safe point of observation. We won't get within ten miles of an Indian. Do you observe that no flies cling to my person? (*They join* SOPHIA.)

(Enter JOHNNIE, *dragging in* CADWALLADER, R. U. E.)

JOHN. Come on, Cad. We'll do 'em! We'll do 'em! Hooray! We'll do 'em! Whoop! I'm the whirling blizzard of the wild and woolly — blood in me eye, whatter ye soy — say, got yer gun?

CAD. Ya-as. *(Takes tiny pistol from vest pocket.)*

JOHN. O mamma! Look at the rifled cannon! Look at it! Say, if you shoot a man with that thing you want to break for cover.

CAD. Aw — why?

JOHN. 'Cause if he found it out he'd whale the stuffing out of you! Sizz — boom — ah-h! *(Exit,* L. I E.)

BIGGS *(down* C.). Come, lieutenant.

CAD. *(hesitating).* You're quite, *quite,* QUITE sure that we — aw — wun no wisk?

BIGGS. No risk whatever.

CAD. *(lights cigarette).* Aw, thanks.

BIGGS. Those cussed cigarettes would protect you anyhow. *(Sniffing.)* Indians can't stand everything. *(Exit with* CADWALLADER, L. I E.)

(Enter MAMIE, R. U. E., *followed by* SEGURA *and* RETTA.)

MAM. Oh, dear, oh, dear, *oh,* dear! They're both going away to get killed!

MRS. B. *(down* C.). So is Jeremiah!

MAM. And they'll get shot all full of great big ho-ho-holes!

MRS. B. And the Indians will cut off their h-h-heads!

MAM. And I'll *bet* they'll get killed!

MRS. B. I'm shoo-shoo-shoo-sure of it!

MAM. But I won't cry.

MRS. B. Me neither.

BOTH. Boo hoo-hoo! *(Embracing.)*

MRS. B. Don't c-c-cry, dear.

MAM. I ain't going to!

MRS. B. Me neither!

BOTH *(as before).* Boo-hoo-hoo! *(They embrace and go up* C.)

SOPH. (L.). Mamie.

MAM. (L.). Yes, dear.

SEG. *(down* R. *to* RETTA). What do you think of my scheme?

RET. It is magnificent — and yet —

SEG. *(impatiently).* And yet? And what? *(Music louder.)*

RET. Nothing. *(Music — brisk march.)*

MRS. B. *(at back).* Look! There they go!

MAM. *(clapping hands).* There's the colonel! Hooray! *(Waves handkerchief.)*

RET. And there is Paul!

SOPH. (L. C.). Paul! Paul! Come — come back! Ah! (*Drops fainting,* L. C.)

SEG. (*to* RETTA). See! Your revenge has begun! (*Music swells.*)

CURTAIN.

ACT III.

SCENE. — *Same as first act, except that curtains are drawn and a lighted lamp is on table. Lights partly down. Landscape as seen through windows at first shows moonlight effects which grow fainter and gradually change to sunlight. This act begins before dawn of the third day. Discover* RETTA *at window,* L. MRS. BIGGS *is in arm-chair up* R., *while* MAMIE *sits at her feet pillowing her head in her lap. Both are asleep. Soft and plaintive music at rise of curtain.*

RET. (*dropping curtain and turning away*). Oh, the long and weary night! Will it never end? And when the gray dawn comes, what news will it bring — victory or defeat, life or death? They are asleep. (*Looks off* L. U. E.) And she, too, is sleeping at last, worn out with weary watching. (*Down* L.) But I cannot rest, nor sleep. (*Sits* L., *front.*) I so longed, so prayed for revenge; but now that I have gained it through the dreadful wrong I did her and him, how poor and weak it is, and how wretched it has made me! They say that revenge is sweet. It is a lie, for revenge is bitter as wormwood. (*Rising.*) I can not, I will not endure it. I will awaken her and tell her everything. (*Goes up* L.) But no. (*Pausing.*) He may have fallen, and then her pity for me will turn to loathing. O Mother in heaven, what shall I do, what shall I do? (*Sinks into chair near window, overcome with emotion.*)

MAM. (*waking*). Ah-h! (*Yawns.*) Oh, dear! Ouch! I've broken my neck. Mrs. Bi — (*yawns*) iggs! Mrs. Biggs, wake up!

MRS. B. Heh? A-oh, I wasn't asleep. (*Yawns.*)

MAM. Neither was (*yawns*) I — much.

MRS. B. It must be near morning.

MAM. (*looking at watch*). Yes, it's four o'clock.

MRS. B. Poor Mr. Biggs! I know he's killed.

MAM. Yes, and poor Lieut. Cadwallader, I know he's scared to death.

MRS. B. I shall be a poor, lone widow. (*Crying.*)

MAM. I won't even have that consolation, and I look just divine in black.

MRS. B. Think of poor Mr. Biggs sleeping there on the cold ground without his nightcap.

MAM. And think of the poor lieutenant, out there fighting Indians and getting killed, without a chance to comb his hair or even put on a clean collar.

MRS. B. It must be growing light. Come out on the veranda and see if any one is stirring. Those *pesky* Indians! I wish they were all dead.

MAM. They might be, if we had only sent them enough rum and missionaries. (*Exit with* MRS. B., C. D.)

RETTA (*rising and looking through window*). The dawn is breaking. A faint, rosy glow lights up the distant mountains, but the earth looks dark and ghostly under the waning moonbeams. (*Drops curtain.*) And my soul is dark — dark as the heavy midnight. Look where I may, I can see no ray of light, no gleam of hope. (*Down* C.) Where shall I go? what can I do? A few hours ago I was as happy as the merry bird that sings beside my window; and now I am miserable as a spirit of darkness, shut out forever from light and joy and peace. (*Seated*, R.) Ah (*shivers*), what is the matter? What is it? I am cold — cold — as if an icy blast of winter was sweeping through the room. Oh! (*Rising.*) My heart feels like lead. I am numb, choking — ah! (*Faints, dropping into chair*, R.)

(*Enter* SOPHIA, L. U. E.)

SOPH. (*running to* RETTA). Retta (*kneeling beside her*)! Retta! Retta! Oh! is she dead? Retta! What shall I do? (*Raises her head.*) Speak to me, dear! can't you?

RET. (*dazed*). What is the matter?

SOPH. You were over-excited, nervous, frightened — as we all are at this time.

RET. And I fainted?

SOPH. Yes, dear.

RET. How thoughtless of me!

SOPH. Thoughtless?

RET. Yes — and selfish; for I disturbed your rest.

SOPH. Poor dear! what a good, kind heart you have!

RET. I? Oh, don't —

SOPH. And I have really been cruel enough to think ill of you. Forgive me, dear.

RET. Forgive you? Nay, it is I who should ask forgiveness. It is I who should kneel at your feet and humbly beg for mercy.

SOPH. Retta!

RET. Scorn me, hate me if you will, pity me if you can; but don't be kind to me. No, no, no; it makes me hate myself.

SOPH. Poor child! You have nothing to regret. You could not know that he was playing me false; and even if you had known of it, the blame was not your own.

RET. (*aside*). She finds ready words to excuse me. But what would she say if — dare I, dare I tell her? If you knew —

SOPH. I do know that you have been sadly, shamefully wronged. (RETTA *weeps.*) But don't feel so badly. There will yet be sunshine and joy for you. He cannot be entirely heartless. And when they return —

RET.   Perhaps they never will return.

SOPH.   Oh, yes; they will.   My father is an experienced officer, and he said it might be only a brief skirmish.   Besides, your— your—

RET.   Uncle?   Don't speak of him.   I am almost wicked enough to hope that I may never see *him* again.

SOPH.   (*aside*).   I don't think that would be anything very wicked.

(*Enter* MRS. BIGGS *and* MAMIE, C. D.)

MRS. B.   Oh-h!   Some one is coming.

SOPH.   Who is it?

MRS. B.   I don't know; a man, or — a — something.

MAM.   I'm just dead sure it's something.   (RETTA *and* SOPHIA *go up* L.)

MRS. B.   D-d-don't be frightened.

MAM.   I'm n-n-not — are y-y-you?

MRS. B.   Not a bit.   I — o-o-ch!   (*Runs* R.)

MAM.   Oh-h!   (*Runs* L.)

(*Enter* CADWALLADER, C. D., *without hat, clothing torn, eye blackened, face scratched, and generally used up.*)

MAM.   There!   It's the lieutenant.   I knew they'd kill him.

CAD.   (*dropping into chair*).   Ya-as — we're all killed.

MAM.   Are you dead?

MRS. B.   Are you hurt?

RET.   Where is Paul?

SOPH.   Where is father?

MAM.   Where is Johnnie?

MRS. B.   Where is Jeremiah?

ALL.   *Where are they?*

CAD.   Ya-as — I suppose so.

MAM.   How many did you kill?

CAD.   How many what?

ALL.   Indians!

CAD.   Blawst the Indians!   I haven't seen any.   (*General disgust.*)

RET.   Then what is the matter with you?

CAD.   Mattah?   Dooce it all, I'm a weck — a total weck.

MAM.   You look it.

CAD.   Ya-as; I look weal dweadful, don't I?

MRS. B.   You wretch!   What have you done with my Jeremiah?

CAD.   And what has youah Jewemiah done with me?   Led me astway, wuined me complexion, spoiled me clothes!   D-d-*damn* youah Jewemiah!   (*Exit* MRS. BIGGS, *indignantly*, C. D.)

MAM.   Tell us all about it, that's a dear.   (SOPHIA *and* RETTA *go up* L. *and exit*, L. U. E.)

CAD.   I cawn't wemembah much, don't you know.

MAM.   (*impatiently*).   Well, well!

CAD. Ya-as. We followed the men foh a time, at a distance —
MAM. Of course ; go on !
CAD. We did. It was awfully hot, and the men got way ahead
of us, and by and by we heard some shooting, and a gwate, big
wabbit spwang up in the path and fwightened the ponies, and his
wan *that* way and mine wan *this* way —
MAM. Toward the fort ?
CAD. Ya-as. Then I lost command of the bwute, and I also
lost me hat and me eyeglasses and me walking-stick, and — and
me cigawettes ! Wasn't it shocking ?
MAM. Paralyzing. And then — keep it up — and then ?
CAD. The next thing I knew me feet got out of the stirrups, and
I had to hang on awound the pony's neck. Then suddenly he
stopped.
MAM. Well — go on.
CAD. (*dolefully*). I did.
MAM. You did ?
CAD. Ya-as. Look at me. (*Rising and turning around.*)
MAM. Then what ?
CAD. Nothing, foh I landed on me head.
MAM. That was lucky.
CAD. I beg to diffah. It disturbed me bwains, which is some-
thing I *nevah* do meself ; besides that, I had to walk back, and I
lost me way, and I know I shall be a weck all me life.
MAM. Oh, no, you won't. With a few more such adventures,
you will develop into a thoroughbred cow — er —
CAD. Aw —
MAM. — boy ; cowboy.
CAD. (*half rising*). Oh !
MAM. What's the matter ?
CAD. (*seated*). A — a cwick in the back.
MAM. Here — take a bracer. (*Pours liquor from flask.*)
CAD. What is it ?
MAM. Hardware — dynamite — earthquake — whiskey.
CAD. Is it stwong ?
MAM. You tell.
CAD. It's got a bad look (*smells*), and it smells awfully dead.
MAM. Never mind ; shut your eyes and let her go. Now — all
ready — one — two —
CAD. Say, if anything happens, send me home on ice. (*Drinks.*)
Ah, I don't wondah they kill people out in this country. (*Attempts
to rise.*) Oh, my ! Blawst it !
MAM. Let me help you.
CAD. Thanks awfully. (*She helps him to his feet.*)
MAM. Steady now. Brace up. Lean on me.
CAD. Thanks aw — oh ! awfully. If you'd only let me lean on
you through life.
MAM. (*aside*). Oh, my lord ! Whew !
CAD. I mean it — 'pon honah, I do.

MAM. Stuff! You don't care a row of pins for me.

CAD. Aw — but I do. I love you evah and evah and *evah* so much. If you'll only agwee, I'll do anything you say.

MAM. Ah! Will you talk United States?

CAD. Ya–as.

MAM. Then say "*yes.*"

CAD. Yes.

MAM. Will you dress like an American?

CAD. Ya — yes.

MAM. Will you throw away your fool walking-stick, single-barrel eyeglass, and cigarettes?

CAD. Aw — well — I —

MAM. Well, what?

CAD. Well, ya — yes.

MAM. And you'll try to *think* now and then?

CAD. It's no use. I see you won't have me. I *cawn't* think. I wasn't built that way.

MAM. No matter. I'll think for you.

CAD. Thanks! Thanks awfully. Then you'll have me?

MAM. Ya-as!

CAD. Eureka! I don't know who he was, but (*embracing her*) it's something awfully jolly.

(*Enter* BIGGS, C. D. *Like* CADWALLADER, *he is much the worse for wear.*)

BIGGS. So — you've got back, have you?

CAD. No, I haven't; have you?

BIGGS. Don't you be impudent, sir!

MAM. (*to* CAD.). Go it! I'll back you!

CAD. Thanks — aw — give me some more of that earthquake. (*Drinks.*)

BIGGS. What did you run off and leave me for, you cowardly snob?

CAD. You — ah — (*Drinks.*)

MAM. (*nudging him*). That's right. Sail in!

CAD. And what did *you* wun — run — off and leave *me* for, you antiquated old — old — devil?

MAM. Oh, glory! He's learning to swear! — Go it now! Go it!

BIGGS. Antiquated, sir! Antiquated! I'll — I'll — burr!

CAD. So'll I burr-r-r! (*Excited business.* CADWALLADER *drinks.*)

(*Enter* MRS. BIGGS, C. D.)

MRS. B. (*embracing* BIGGS). O Mr. Biggs! O Jeremiah! And you are really, really, truly, really not dead?

BIGGS. No; but there will be a really, truly dead dude here (CAD. *drinks*) in just about an infinitesimal fraction of time, if you will only get out of the way!

MRS. B. (*clinging to him*). No, no, Jeremiah.

CAD. That's wight. Cling to Jewemiah, unless you want me to spattah him all ovah this woom.

BIGGS. (*struggling*). Let me get at him for a moment — a single moment !

CAD. (*to* MAMIE). D-d-do you suppose she will ?

MAM. Never. You're safe. Roast him !

CAD. Why don't you come on — you old Egyptian obelisk ? (*Drinks.*) You ossified mummy ! Come on — ic — you cowardly old conundrum !

BIGGS. Mrs. Biggs, I command you !

MRS. B. (*standing aside*). Well, then, if you're bound to fight —

MAM. All ready for the first round ! (*Pushes* CADWALLADER *toward* BIGGS, *who retreats.*)

BIGGS. I — ahem ! On due consideration, and mature reflection, the immediate presence of the gentler sex induces me to allow you to remain *in statu quo* for the present time being. But beware, sir ! beware of the aftermath. You have aroused the sleeping lion, and his roar will reverberate to the uttermost heights of the towering Magdalena Mountains.

CAD. (*half aside*). Ya-as. You *can* hear a jackass a long way —ic—way.

BIGGS. I scorn to bandy words with you, sir. Come, Mrs. Biggs. Let us hence to our own domicile. In due time, sir, you may expect to find your *disjecta membra* scattered all over New Mexico, and to be fined fifty thousand dollars for contempt of court. (*At* C. D.) In the language of the poet — (MRS. BIGGS *pulls his arm*) damn it, let me alone ! (*Exit with* MRS. BIGGS C. D.)

CAD. (*slightly tipsy*). Well ? How'm I doing ? Firs' — ic — rate ?

MAM. You're a holy terror !

CAD. Bet—yer—life. Dander's up. No more dud f' me ; ic — bad man !

MAM. Correct. Now go to your room and sober up.

CAD. All ri', all r:'. Didn' I do 'im ? Bad — ic — bad man ! Blood 'n m' eye ! Wah ! Oop ! (*Exit*, R. U. E.)

MAM. It's a modern miracle. A dude turned into a man. I believe that he will be really plucky when he gets his blood up.

(*Enter* JOHNNIE, *quickly*, C. D.)

JOHN. Blood ! Who wants blood ? Trot him out ! I'm right in the business, I am. Yah ! I'm the wild-eyed avenger ! the unterrified scourge of the plains ! You hear me scream ?

MAM. Jonathan Bangs !

JOHN. Correct. That's me — right side up with care, and hungry as a tramp. Oh, I tell you that was a gorgeous battle. Ping ! Bang ! Puff ! And over they went !

MAM.   Put up that horrid gun.   It might go off.

JOHN.   It has, no end of times, and it did fearful execution.

(*Enter* SEGURA, C. D.)

MAM.   Yes — shot some more cows perhaps.

SEG.   Only a mule or two, Miss Bangs.   The colonel stopped him before he did any serious damage.

MAM.   (*laughing*).   O Johnnie!

JOHN.   Well, I shot *at* one Injun anyhow.

SEG.   So I observed.   But, as he was a mile away, he was not badly injured.

MAM.   Then there was no battle?

SEG.   Only a trifling skirmish.

JOHN.   That was all.   We did 'em just too easy — we did! (*Exit*, R. U. E.)

MAM.   No battle!   The idea!   So we had our long fright all for nothing.   Where are the soldiers?

SEG.   They will soon be here.

MAM.   I'll tell Sophia; but I think it's a real awful shame that you didn't get killed — at least a little bit — so now! (*Exit*, L. U. E.)

SEG.   The devil you do!   She is a pleasant creature — if anything a little *too* pleasant.   Um!   I expect a breeze when Wybert returns.   Curse the young cub!   I hope he won't oblige me to kill him — at least at present.

(*Enter* SOPHIA *and* RETTA, L. U. E.)

RET.   (*down* C.).   Uncle!

SEG.   Good-morning, my dear.   I hope you have slept well.

RET.   Do you, indeed?

SEG.   And why not?   You surely had nothing to fear for me, and (*meaningly*) you certainly cared nothing for the fate of any one else.

RET.   But I —

SEG.   Yes, I see; you have been assuming pity for her; that is right.   You are doing nobly. (RETTA *goes* R. SOPHIA *comes down*.)   Miss Sophia — your devoted.

SOPH.   My father —

SEG.   Will soon be here.

RET.   And is — is —

SEG.   Is he wounded?   Not in the least.

RET.   And is —

SEG.   Is there any limit to your questions?   I dare say not. (*Aside to* RETTA.)   Hold your tongue.   *He* is safe enough, curse him!   I will not have you awaken her interest by any of your stupid questions. (SOPHIA *draws curtains, admitting early sunlight; puts out lamp; lights all up*.)

RET.   But she must be anxious.

SEG.   She better not.

RET.   And why ?

SEG.   Because she is my promised wife —

RET.   *Your* promised wife ?

SEG.   And shall harbor no thoughts of him.

RET.   Your — promised — wife !

SEG.   Yes, and yes again ; and still yes and yes. My plan is working grandly. When Wybert arrives, you must welcome him with the utmost affection. Be as loving as you please. He will not repulse you, and *she* will not interfere.

RET.   What have you done with that forged paper ?

SEG.   *Forged* paper ?

RET.   Yes ; the — the one I signed.

SEG.   Ah ! you mean your marriage certificate.

RET.   Yes — that shameful —

SEG.   Of course ; he *is* a shameful fellow. But I shall expose him.

RET.   Expose *him ?*   Uncle, let us have an understanding. You are —

SEG.   Exactly.   I am — managing this affair (*grasping her arm*), and be careful that you make no mistake in your work ; for if you do (*meaningly*), it will be a very expensive mistake for you, my dear.

RET. (*aside*). Demon that he is! What new villany is he planning ?   (*Goes up* R. *and exits,* R. U. E.)

SEG. (L.). Daylight at last ! Ah, my dear Sophia, how pleasant the sunshine is after a long and dreary night. And yet, to me, the past night has been a joyous, happy dream.

SOPH.   To me it has been a terrible reality.

SEG.   The anxiety you felt — regarding your father — was natural, of course.

SOPH.   If that were all —

SEG.   Then I, too, have had a place in your thoughts?   I thank you truly, for you have lifted an oppressive doubt from my mind.

SOPH.   A doubt ?

SEG.   Yes ; for I had thought — you will pardon me, I am sure — that you had, possibly, accepted me in a moment of pique ; and that — pardon me again — you might be weak enough to hold a lingering regard for the — ah — person — who had so brutally trifled with your affections.

SOPH.   Señor !

SEG.   I see that I was wrong. Forgive me. I should have known that such a thought was unjust to a girl like you. My poor niece would grovel at his feet ; but you — ah, your splendid American spirit will not submit to insult. You cannot forget that he has made your heart his plaything ; that the honeyed words whispered in your ear were but the echo of words spoken to others ; that his self-conceit rejoiced at the thought of adding you to the number of his abject worshippers ; and that —

SOPH.   No more — no more ; I cannot bear it.

SEG. Then you do not regret your promise to me?

SOPH. I regret nothing, except that I ever saw him. (*Music: lively march, off* L. U. E. *Low at first, then louder.* SOPHIA *crosses* L.)

SEG. (*aside*). Jealousy raises the devil, especially with women. (*Aloud.*) The regiment has returned. And now, my dear Sophia, may I tell your father of my happiness, and ask his consent to our marriage?

SOPH. (*quickly*). No — please — not yet. Give me a little time — I —

SEG. But think how anxious I am; and besides, he ought to know.

SOPH. Yes — he shall — but give me a little time, for I — I —

(*Enter* RETTA, C. D. *from* R.)

RET. O Sophia! Here comes your father! (SOPHIA *starts up.*) And Paul too!

SOPH. Oh! (*Comes down and sits* L.)

SEG. (*aside*). There! one of them waiting to fly *to* him, and the other waiting to fly *at* him. O woman, woman, woman! What a precious fool you are! (*Exit,* R. U. E.)

(*Enter* LAWTON *and* PAUL, C. D.)

LAW. Sophia, my child!

SOPH. (*embracing him*). Father!

LAW. Bless my soul! What *is* the matter?

SOPH. Nothing, only — I — I am so glad you have returned.

LAW. Yes, safe and sound. But there! Paul is waiting. (*Goes* L.)

SOPH. (*glancing at* RETTA). And so is some one else.

PAUL. Indeed? (*Looks at* RETTA, *who is timidly regarding him. Then, indignant at* SOPHIA, *comes down and takes* RETTA'S *hand.*) You, at least, will welcome me back. You are glad to see me, are you not?

RET. Yes, I am glad to see you. (*They go* R.)

LAW. (*looking around*). Hello! Well, of all things! What does that mean?

SOPH. Let him answer. (*Crosses* L.)

LAW. (C.). Why — I — look here — the Devil! (*Aside.*) No, sir! The poet is all wrong. (*At* C. D.) The "proper study of mankind" is — woman. And the more you learn of her, the less you really know. (*Exit,* C. D.)

PAUL. So, you see, the outbreak really amounted to nothing. But there, I must leave you now.

RET. Wait; I have not told you.

PAUL. Never mind, Retta. You are a good, warm-hearted girl, for (*significantly*) you did not become an icicle on my return.

SOPH. (*aside*). That is for *my* benefit.

PAUL. There is no frost in your nature. You could never freeze a man's heart as some of your northern sisters delight in doing.

SOPH. (*indignantly*). No; but she can burn her poor heart out for a wretch who is unworthy of her slightest thought.

PAUL. And that same fire may warm a frozen heart into life, and thus disappoint somebody.

SOPH. And if *somebody's* sword was as sharp as his tongue, what a soldier he would make !

PAUL (*at* C. D.). An excellent suggestion. That sword will receive immediate attention. (*Exit*, C. D.)

SOPH. (*aside*). I could fairly cry my eyes out if she were not here.

RET. Sophia —

SOPH. Yes, dear.

RET. I am going away.

SOPH. Why should you?

RET. You will not wonder when I tell you. Since I came here I have brought only sorrow to you, to him, to myself. But before I go I must tell you of the dreadful wrong I have done you both.

SOPH. Retta!

RET. Don't touch me; don't come near me. Only listen. Yesterday my heart was filled with bitterness toward you. I was consumed with jealous rage, mad with envious spite. I hated him: I hated you both. In my eagerness for vengeance I thus endeavored to separate you by every art known to a desperate, wicked woman. That scene which you witnessed between us was innocent of all wrong on his part. Trapped into a promise he gave the kiss you saw — as I well knew — and could explain nothing without breaking his word. You have all been so good, so kind, to me, and I — oh, what a miserable wretch I am! (*Sinks into chair* R., *sobbing*.)

SOPH. (*kneeling beside her*). Poor, wayward child! What has my suffering been compared to yours?

RET. But mine are all deserved. O Sophia! can you ever forgive me?

SOPH. (*kissing her*). With all my heart.

RET. And Paul — Capt. Wybert; tell him all that I have said. Be happy — happy — and forget me.

SOPH. Forget you?

RET. (*returning and embracing her*). No, I don't mean that. Forget the wrong I did, and remember me with all the pity, sorrow, and kindness possible. Good-by. Good-by. (*Exit*, R. U. E.)

SOPH. (*up* C.). Poor Retta! poor child. If there were only *two* Pauls how nice it *would* be! (*Looks off* C. D.) There he goes! Now I *will* surprise him. (*Exit*, C. D. *to* L.)

(*Enter* SEGURA *and* LAWTON, R. U. E.)

LAW. Well, señor, I believe that the trouble is all over, at least for the present.

SEG. With the Indians — yes; but there seems to be a small domestic warfare raging here in the garrison.

LAW. Yes. Women beat the Devil.

SEG. And there is where men have the best of it; for they sometimes beat women.

LAW. I don't see what can possess my daughter.

SEG. I know of some one who hopes to.

LAW. Yes?

SEG. Yes. And your consent, I trust, will not be withheld.

LAW. My consent is evidently of small consequence. Parents are ciphers nowadays. I control my regiment easily, but my daughter —

SEG. Easily controls you.

LAW. Well, I don't deny it. She is all I have on earth, and, bless her heart, never abuses her power.

SEG. Then she will make an admirable wife.

LAW. No doubt; for she and Paul are doing all their quarrelling before marriage.

SEG. *Their* marriage! Whose marriage?

LAW. Sophia and Capt. Wybert's. I supposed you knew.

SEG. I know that she will *not* marry Capt. Wybert.

LAW. Really?

SEG. Really.

LAW. You surprise me.

SEG. Doubtless; but I have my reasons.

LAW. Suppose you name them.

SEG. With pleasure. First, then, your daughter is engaged to me.

LAW. What!

SEG. And why not? I am well born, rich, fairly intelligent, not exactly hideous — unless my mirror lies — and, I am pleased to say, my heart, hand, and fortune have been accepted by your daughter.

LAW. My dear fellow, you certainly are dreaming. My daughter —

SEG. Is a high-spirited girl, quick to resent an insult.

LAW. Insult? What do you mean?

SEG. What I say. My proposal was opportune. When she found that she had been duped, played upon, trifled with, by the man who professed to love her, she bravely cast his contemptible image from her heart, and accepted the love of an honest man. That man is myself!

LAW. Duped? My daughter? Why, man, you must be crazy. Such talk is absolute nonsense. My daughter, I tell you, is engaged to Capt. Wybert.

SEG. She was, I admit, until she discovered his real character.

LAW. I will hear no more. Capt. Wybert is a gentleman, and will marry my daughter.

Seg. Capt. Wybert is a double-dyed scoundrel, and will *not* marry your daughter!

Law. Look here, sir, I have a mind to —

Seg. You want my reason?

Law. (*restraining himself*). Yes; be brief.

Seg. Briefly, then, Capt. Wybert will *not* marry her because he has a wife already!

Law. (*passionately*). Señor Segura! That is a lie! (*Crosses* L.)

Seg. (*half drawing sword*). Eh! (*With an effort.*) You — want — proof?

Law. Yes — and be quick about it.

Seg. Very well. Capt. Wybert was married in Mexico. His wedding was kept a profound secret. I heard of it yesterday for the first time.

Law. And his wife —

Seg. Is my poor, wronged, unhappy niece.

Law. Retta?

Seg. Yes, Retta. If you want more proof, here is her marriage certificate. Look at it; study it; and then tell me if I lie.

Law. (*examining certificate*). Paul Wybert, Capt. U. S. Cavaly, — Retta — You told the truth, señor. I beg your pardon.

Paul (*outside*, L.). Come dear, it's all right now.

Law. The infamous scoundrel! I'll blow his brains out!

Seg. Don't; he would never miss them.

Law. But damn the fellow —

Seg. That is right. Damn him all you please; only, make an example of him. I will tell you my plan. (*Draws* Lawton *towards* R. U. E.) It will take but a moment. (*Exit* Lawton, R. U. E.) Now, you fools, make the most of your time! (*Exit*, R. U. E.)

(*Enter* Paul *and* Sophia, C. D.)

Soph. (*shaking finger playfully*). Own up, now. Aren't you *ashamed* of yourself?

Paul. Ashamed? The — mischief! What for?

Soph. Oh — everything; making me jealous, and all that.

Paul (*aside*). That's the woman of it.

Soph. And only think, Paul, I had really promised to marry that man.

Paul. A promise, so gained, binds nothing.

Soph. What will he say?

Paul. Whatever he pleases.

Soph. What will he do?

Paul. Travel. His health requires a change.

Soph. You will not quarrel with him? Promise me.

Paul. Well — no. I won't quarrel with *him;* but if he quarrels with *me* —

Soph. O Paul!

Paul. Somebody will have an impressive funeral.

(Enter MAMIE *and* CADWALLADER, C. D.)

MAM.   Another funeral?   That makes two.

SOPH.   Two?

MAM.   That's what I said.

SOPH.   Who was the other?

MAM.   A dude.   Caddie killed him.   Didn't you, eh?

CAD.   Ya-as.

MAM.   Eh?

CAD.   I mean "yes."

PAUL (C.).   You look as if you had met with an accident.

CAD. (L.).   Ya — yes.   I have.   I'm engaged to be maw — married.

SOPH. (R.).   To you?

MAM. (R.).   Cert.

SOPH.   I congratulate you.   But isn't he a — a —

MAM.   Not a bit of it.   He's buried the dude, I tell you — sworn off on cigarettes, and is learning the American language.

SOPH.   Wonderful!   How did it happen?

MAM.   Why, you see, he wants a protector, and I have taken the contract.

CAD. (*to* PAUL).   I suppose that blaw — blasted Spaniard will cut up wus — rusty — when he finds that you have cut him out.

PAUL.   I really hope he will.   (*Going* C.)

(Enter LAWTON *and* SEGURA, R. U. E.)

LAW.   Capt. Wybert!

PAUL.   Sir?

LAW.   You will resign your commission and leave the fort within an hour!

PAUL.   Col. Lawton!

LAW. (C.).   No words!   When a man disgraces his uniform, he must lay it aside forever.   You, whom I had looked upon as a son — who was betrothed to my daughter — whose honor I had thought above question — you of all men to be guilty of such contemptible conduct.   I believe I would do right to kill you in your tracks!

PAUL.   Contemptible conduct, sir?   What do you mean?

SEG. (R).   He means that you have dared make love to his daughter, while your own wife was under his roof.   (*Sensation.*)

SOPH.   His wife!

PAUL.   You miserable, devilish liar!   (*Starts toward* SEGURA.)

LAW.   Halt!   (PAUL *stops.*)

PAUL.   But, colonel!   Such a lie —

LAW.   Silence!   He has spoken the truth; for here I hold the certificate of marriage between his niece and yourself, duly signed and witnessed.   The signature is your own —

(*Enter* RETTA, L. U. E.)

SEG. And here comes the poor girl, who will prove it.

PAUL. Retta, will you —

LAW. Silence, sir ! Retta, my child, come here. Look at this paper. (*She takes it.*) Do you know what it is ?

RET. Yes. (*Slowly.*) It is a marriage certificate.

SEG. Exactly.

LAW. Have you seen it before ?

RET. Yes.

SEG. To be sure.

LAW. Is that your own signature ?

RET. Yes.

SEG. Without doubt. See, I told you.

LAW. And then this is a genuine certificate of your marriage to Paul Wybert ?

RET. (*tears paper*). No! For we were never married ! (*General movement.* SOPHIA *embraces* RETTA ; CADWALLADER *embraces* MAMIE ; SEGURA *takes stage to* R. *front.* PAUL *takes position near* C. D.)

LAW. But that certificate —

RET. Is a cowardly, miserable forgery to which in a moment of foolish passion I wickedly lent my name.

SEG. Don't believe her, Col. Lawton. The fool lies.

LAW. Excuse me, but I prefer to look elsewhere for the liar.

SEG. (*aside*). Ah, curse them all !

LAW. I ask your pardon, my boy.

PAUL (*giving hand*). Granted sir, freely.

MAM. The show is over. Come on, Caddy. Ting-a-ling-a-ling ! Down goes the curtain.

CAD. Ya — yes ; just like a play, isn't it ? (*They exit*, C. D.)

SEG. You astonish me, Col. Lawton.

LAW. Possibly. And I shall astonish you in a different way unless you leave at once. This is no place for sneaks nor forgers. (*Exit*, C. D. ; SEGURA *turns and looks at* RETTA.)

RET. (*shrinking and grasping* SOPHIA'S *arm*). Oh !

SOPH. What is it, dear ? Come with me.

SEG. Stop !

SOPH. Sir !

SEG. I am addressing my niece. You will come with me, if you please. (*With meaning.*) I have an interesting account to settle with you.

RET. (*terrified*). I dare not go.

SEG. Come !

RET. He will murder me.

PAUL (*down* C). No, he will not. You shall remain here.

SEG. Dare you interfere with me ?

PAUL. At any time, sir !

(*Enter* BIGGS *and* JOHNNIE, C. D.)

BIGGS. Here — stop this quarrel. I'll fine you a thousand dollars.

SEG. Go to the devil, you old fool !

BIGGS. Wh-at ! I'll fine *you* a million—

JOHN. Oh, dry up! (*Pushes him to* R. U. E.)

SEG. (*to* RETTA). Come, I tell you.

PAUL (*stopping her*). Remain here. And, as for you (*to* SEGURA), if you leave at once you will avoid the unpleasant sensation of being kicked out. (*Turns away contemptuously.*)

SEG. Ah ! (*Draws knife, rushes at* PAUL, *and strikes. At the same instant* RETTA *throws herself between them and receives the blow.*)

PAUL. Scoundrel ! (*Catches* RETTA *in left arm and knocks* SEGURA *down with right fist.* BIGGS *and* JOHNNIE *bind and secure him.*)

JOHN. (*drawing pistol*). If you breathe, you're dead ! (PAUL *places* RETTA *in chair,* L. C.)

RET. Paul — are — are you safe ?

PAUL. I am safe, Retta.

RET. Thank — God. Good-by, Paul. It is for the best — all for the best. I cannot see you, Paul — nor her. It is all so — so dark. Good-by — Paul. (*Dies ; picture ; music.*)

SLOW CURTAIN.

www.ingramcontent.com/pod-product-compliance
Lightning Source LLC
Chambersburg PA
CBHW022205020726
47496CB00008B/2890